WILLIAM WONDRISKA

A LONG PIECE OF STRING

chronicle books · san francisco

First Chronicle Books LLC edition published in 2010.

Library of Congress Cataloging-in-Publication Data
Wondriska, William, 1931–
A long piece of string / William Wondriska. — 1st Chronicle Books ed.
p. cm.
Summary: Follows a piece of string through images that correspond
to the letters of the alphabet.
ISBN 978-0-8118-7493-9
[1. String—Fiction. 2. Alphabet. 3. String figures.] I. Title.
PZ7.W842Lo 2010
[E]—dc22
2009038926

Jacket design by Amy E. Achaibou.
Book design by William Wondriska.
Typeset in ATDerek and Garamond.

Manufactured by Toppan Leefung, Da Ling Shan Town,
Dongguan, China, in May 2010.

10 9 8 7 6 5 4 3 2 1

This product conforms to CPSIA 2008.

Chronicle Books LLC
680 Second Street, San Francisco, California 94107

www.chroniclekids.com

FOR MY FAMILY

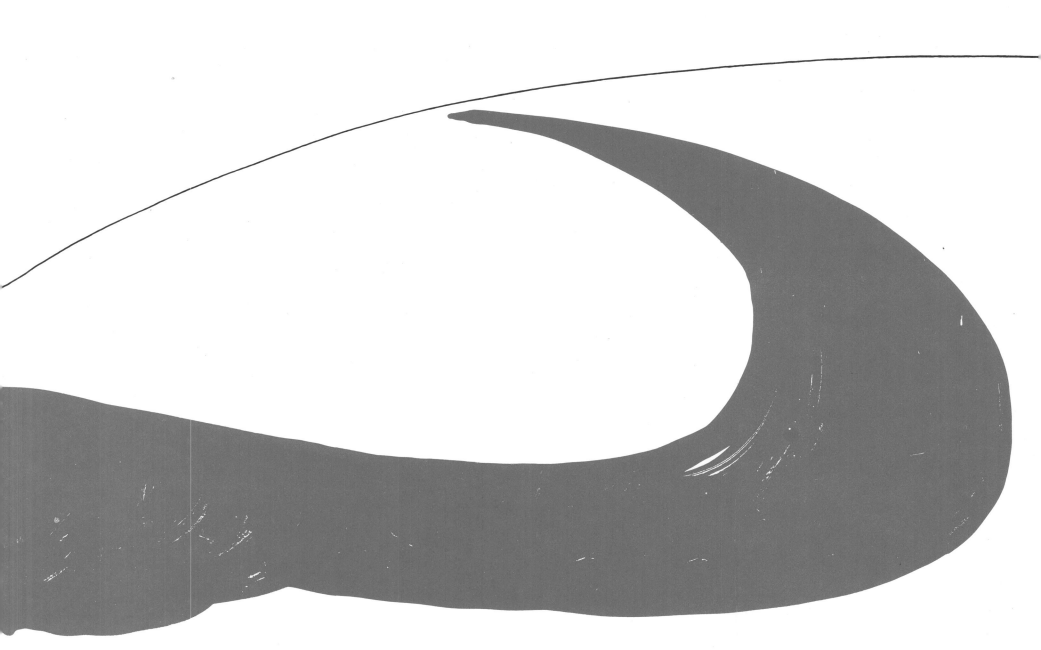

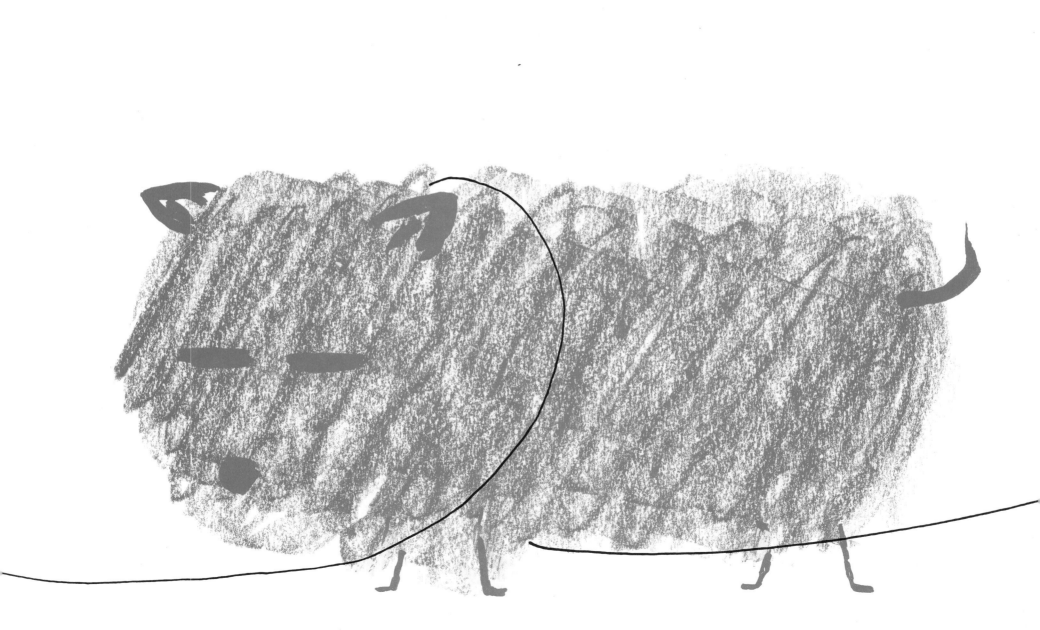

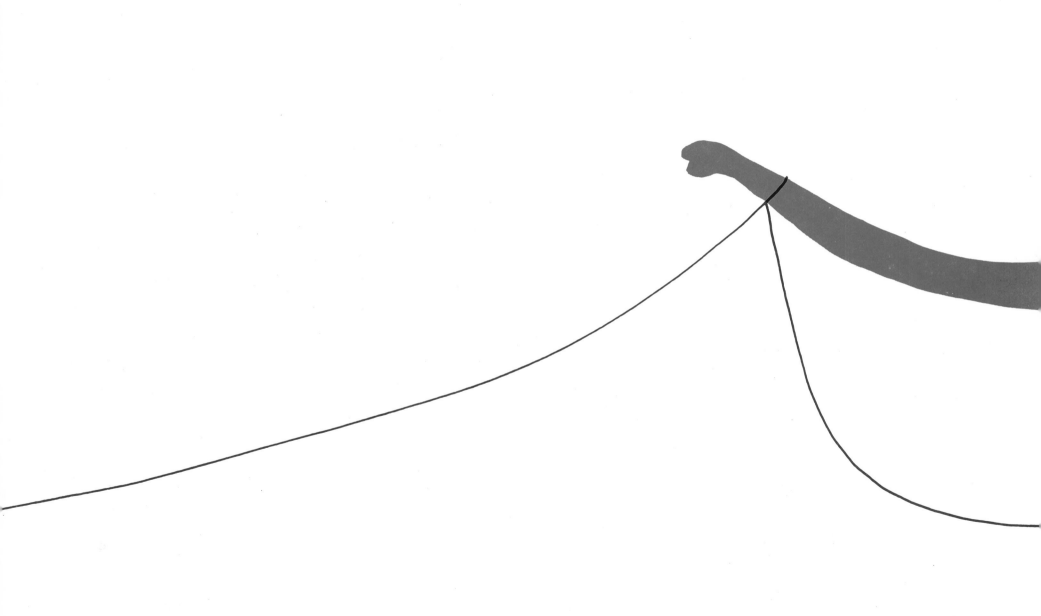

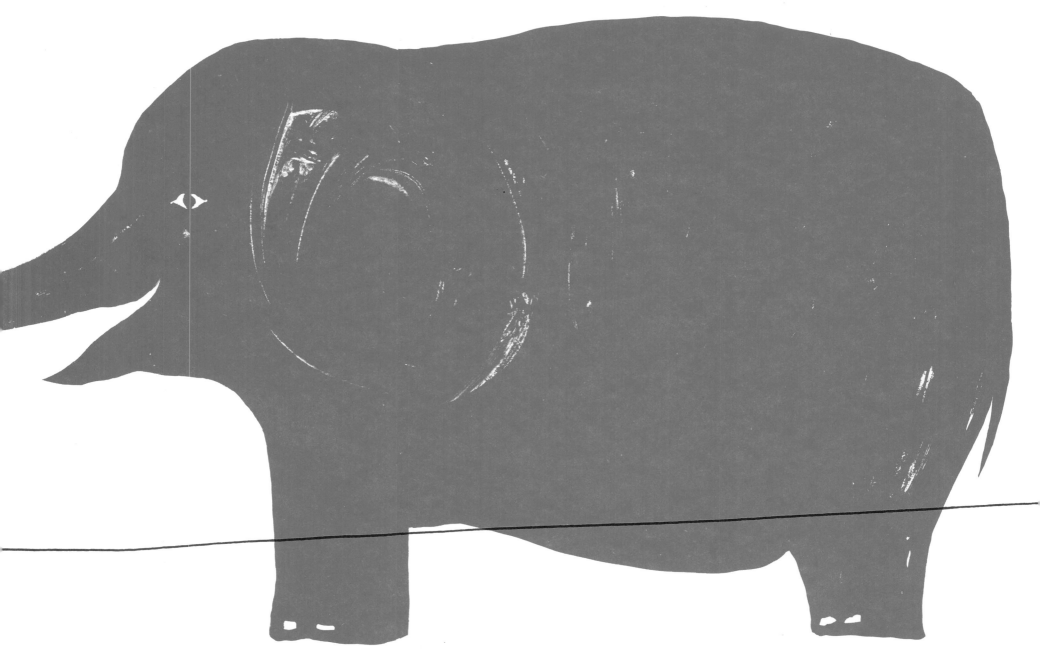

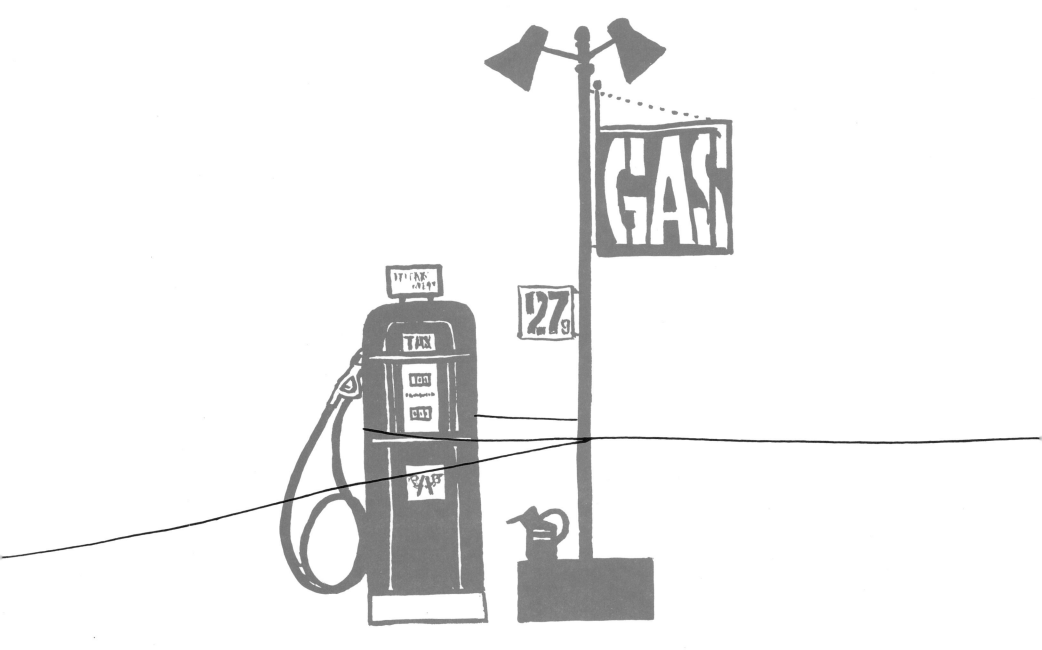

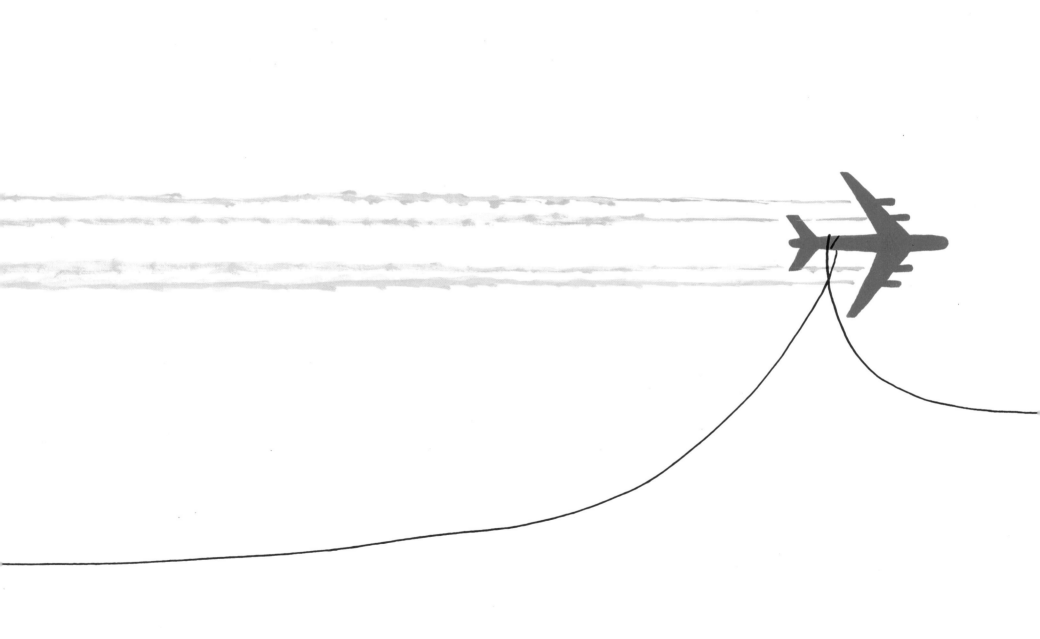

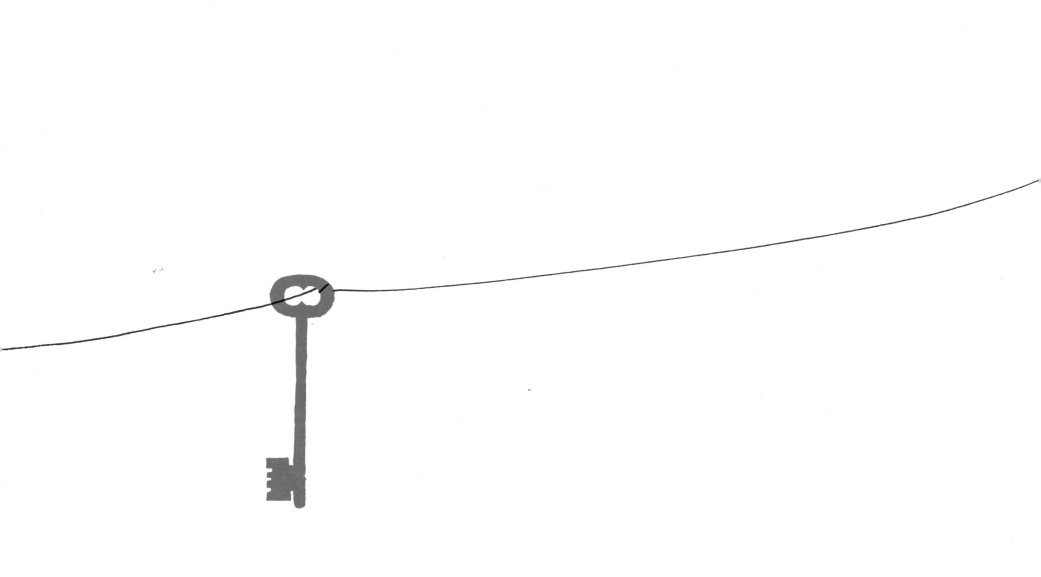

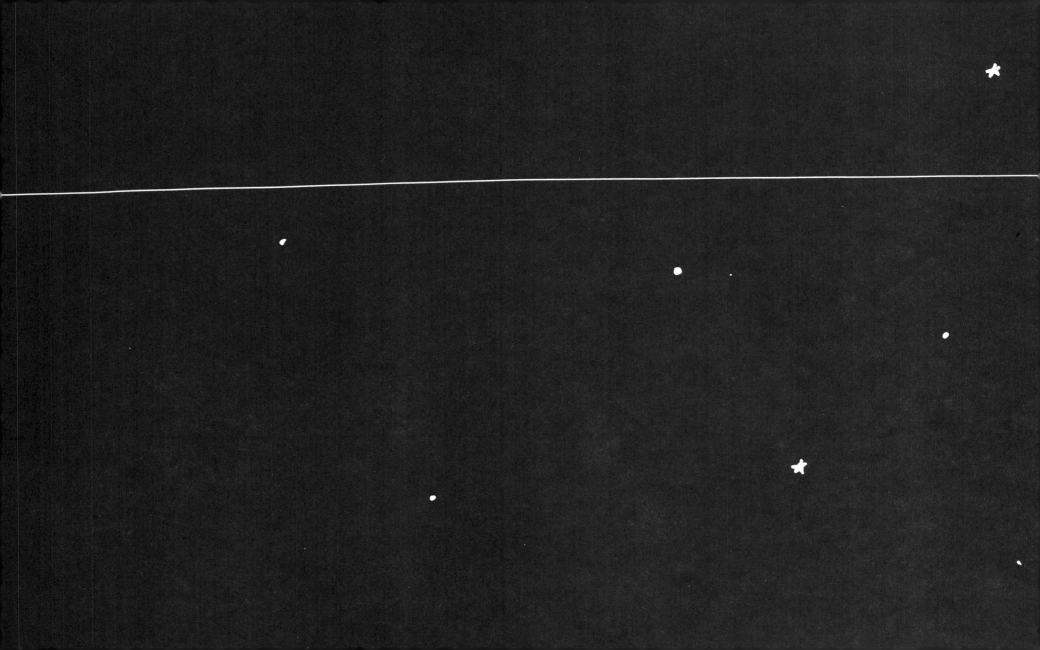

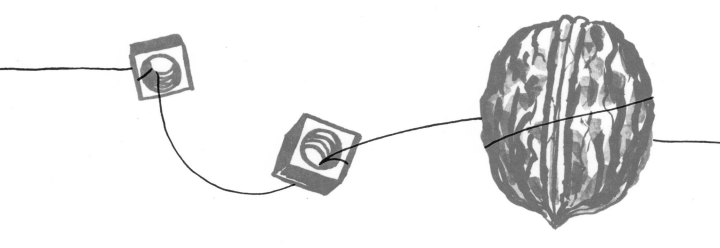

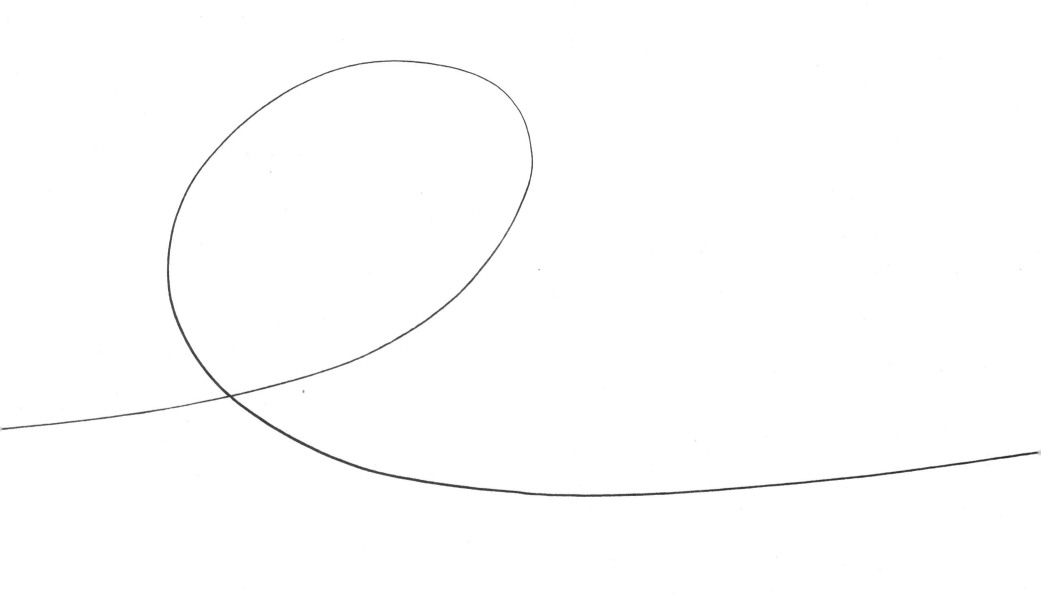

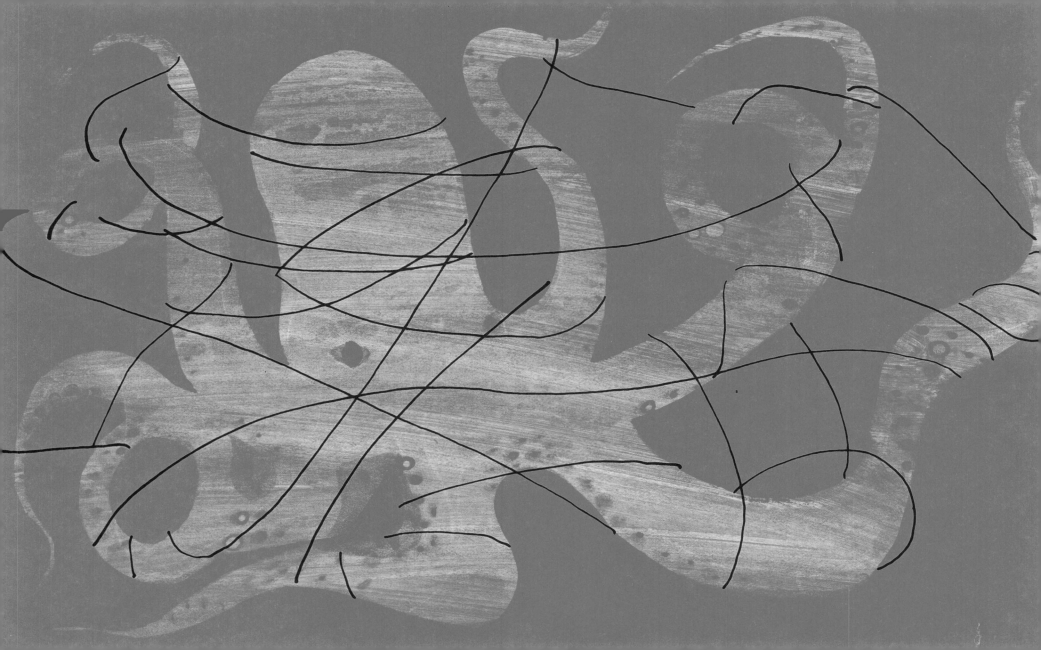

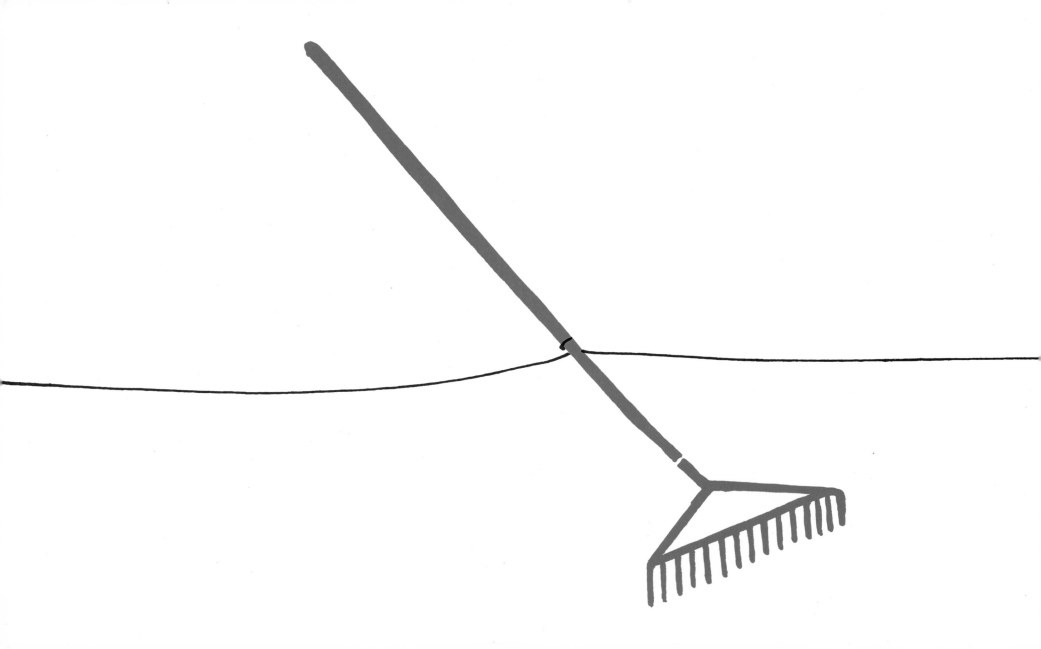

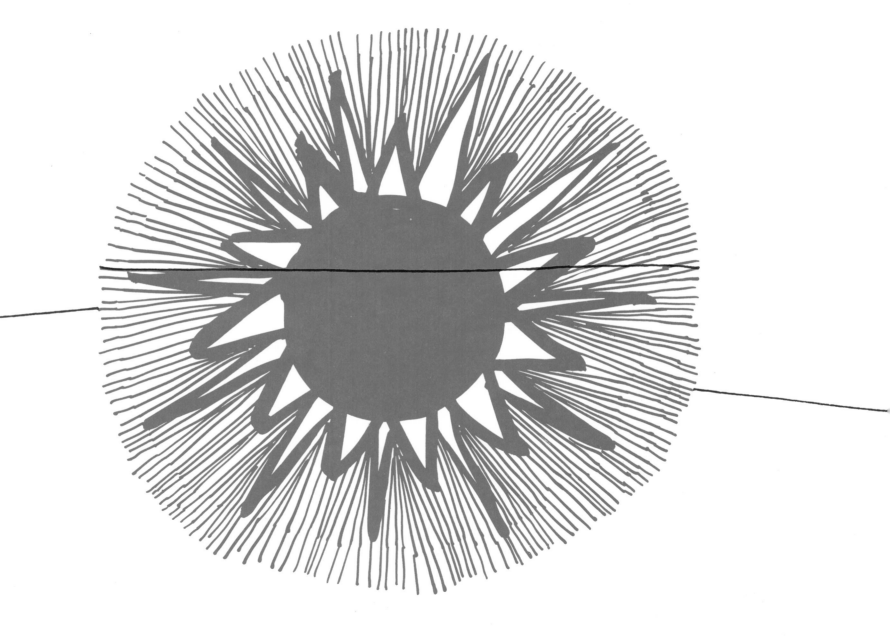

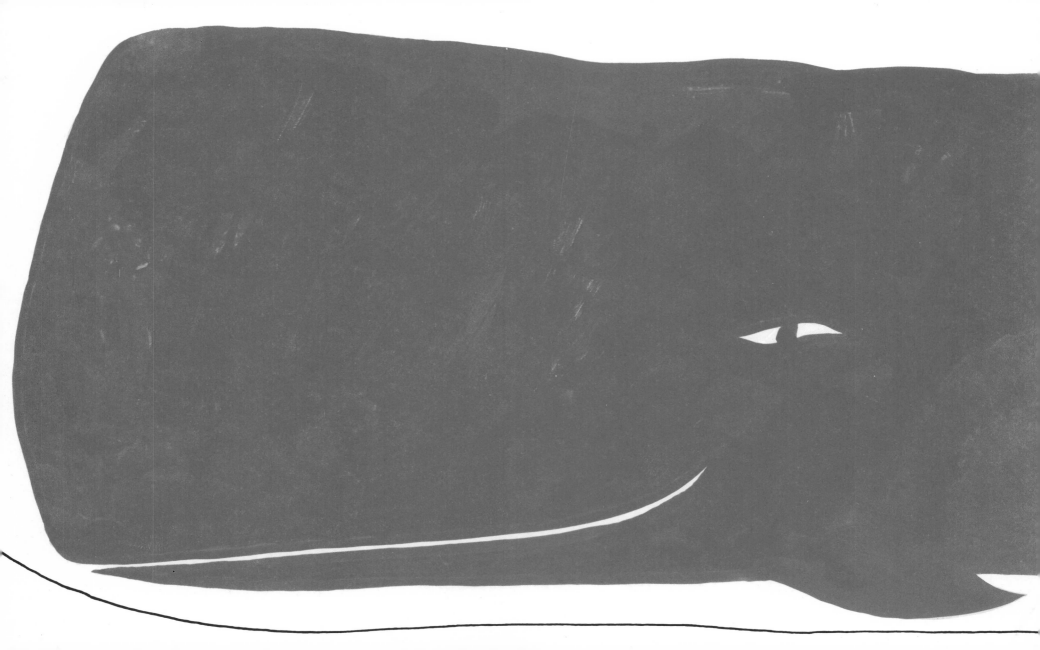

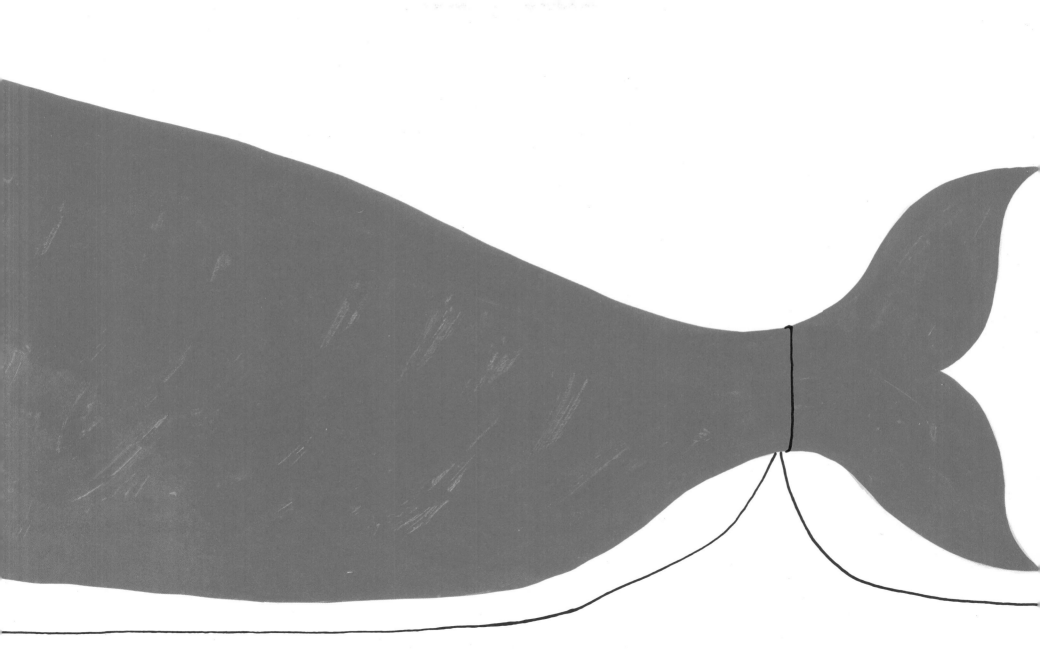

1 22 23 24 25 26 27

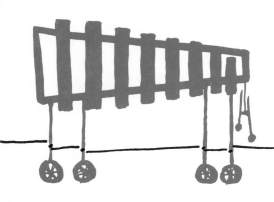

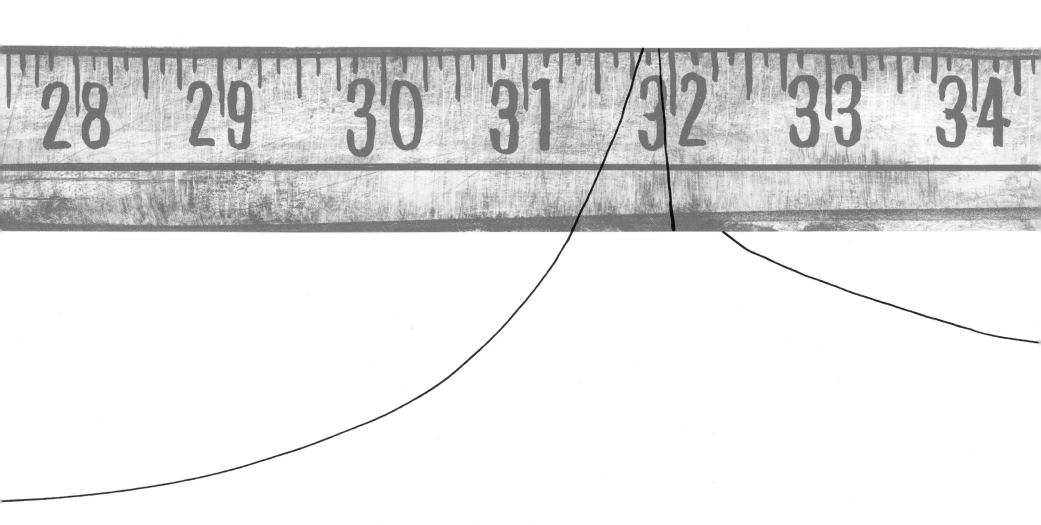

Alligator	**N**uts
Bird	**O**ctopus
Castle	**P**enguin
Dog	**Q**ueen
Elephant	**R**ake
Flower	**S**un
Gas station	**T**rees
House	**U**mbrella
Ice-cream cone	**V**olcano
Jet	**W**hale
Key	**X**ylophone
Leaf	**Y**ardstick
Moon	**Z**ipper

What do you have on your string?

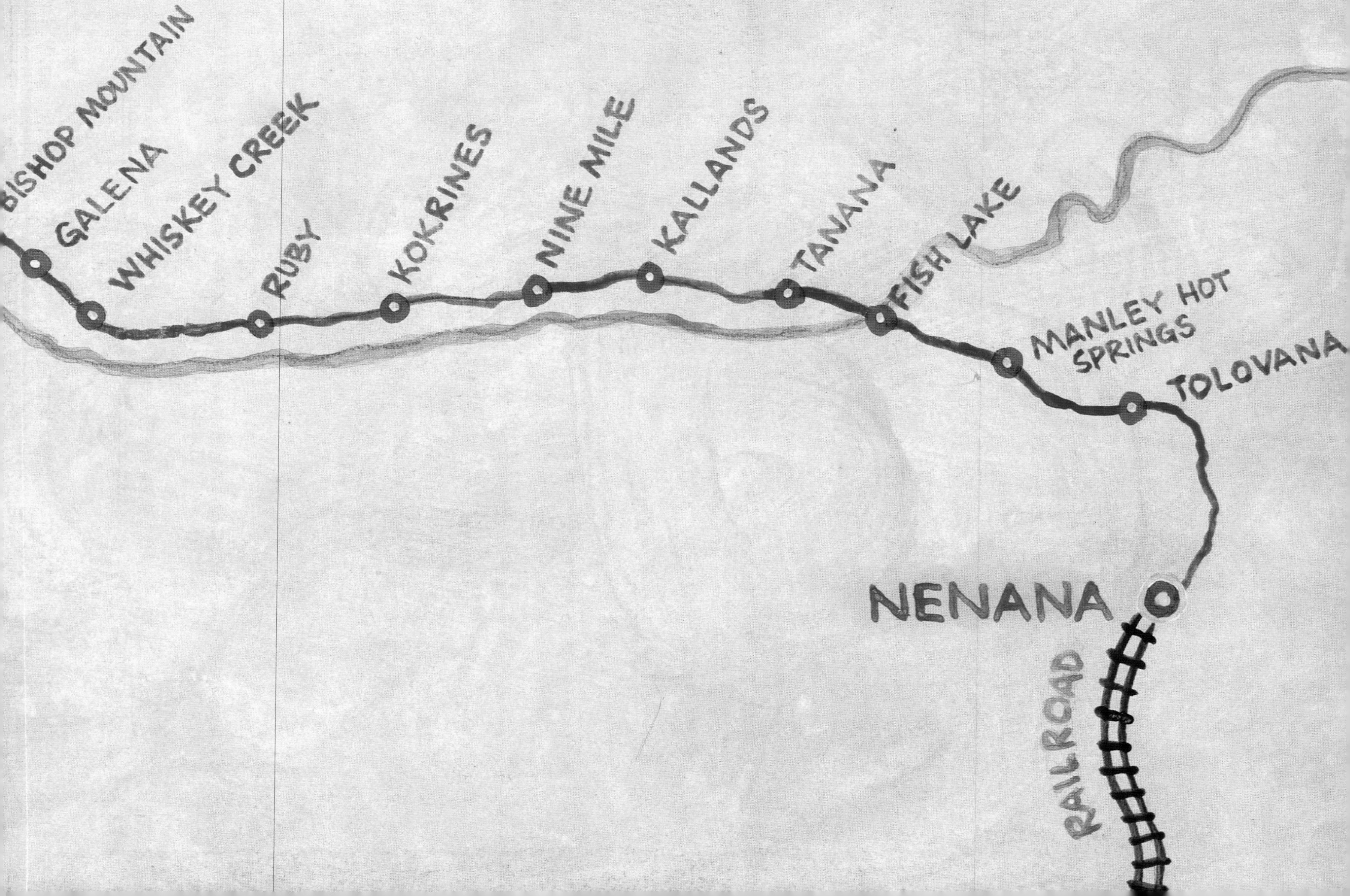

10/06
BISHOP MOUNTAIN
GALENA
WHISKEY CREEK
RUBY
KOKRINES
NINE MILE
KALLANDS
TANANA
FISH LAKE
MANLEY HOT SPRINGS
TOLOVANA
NENANA
RAILROAD

NOME
SAFETY
SOLOMON
BLUFF
GOLOVIN
SHAKTOOLIK
NULATO
KALTAG
UNALAKLEET
OLD WOMAN
YUKON RIVER